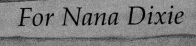

First published in Great Britain by
Andersen Press Ltd in 1995
First published in Picture Lions in 1997
1 3 5 7 9 10 8 6 4 2
ISBN: 0 00 664521 6
Picture Lions is an imprint of the
Children's Division, part of
HarperCollins Publishers Ltd,
77-85 Fulham Palace Road,
Hammersmith, London W6 8JB.
Text and illustrations copyright
© Colin McNaughton 1995
The author/illustrator asserts the
moral right to be identified as the
author/illustrator of the work.
Printed and bound in Hong Kong.

BOO!

Words and Pictures by
Colin McNaughton

PictureLions

An Imprint of HarperCollins*Publishers*

Through the dark, dark streets of the dark, dark town, Preston (the Masked Avenger) sneaks…

"Boo!" says Preston the Masked Avenger and he disappears into the night.

Slinking through the shadows,
Preston the Masked Avenger
spies Billy the Bully,
his next victim...

"Boo!" says Preston the Masked Avenger and he disappears into the night.

Cat-like, Preston the Masked
Avenger slides through the
darkness until he reaches
the school-house
where his teacher
is working late...

"Boo!" says Preston the Masked Avenger and he disappears into the night.

Next, the super-hero
comes to Mr Wolf's house.
"Boo!" says Preston the Masked
Avenger very quietly and
he sneaks right past.
"I may be a super-hero," says
Preston, "but I'm not daft!"
And he disappears
into the night.

Preston the Masked Avenger
lies in wait for the greatest
villain in the universe - his dad.

"Boo!" says Preston the Masked Avenger and he disappears into the night.

(At least, he would have done if his dad hadn't grabbed him first.)

"Preston!" says Preston's dad. "I've had complaints about you from all over town. You're a naughty little pig."

Preston the Unmasked
Avenger is sent to his room
without any supper.

Suddenly!

"Boo!" says Preston's dad.
"That'll teach you to go
around scaring people."

But it doesn't.

COLIN MCNAUGHTON was born in Northumberland and had his first book published while he was still at college. He is now one of Britain's most highly acclaimed authors and illustrators of children's books and a winner of many prestigious awards, including the Kurt Maschler award in 1991.

Boo! is the second hilarious book about Preston the pig. The first, *Suddenly!*, was shortlisted for both the Smarties and the WH Smith/SHE Under-Fives awards.

"For sheer fun and verve, Colin McNaughton is unbeatable."
Radio Times

"Colin McNaughton combines graphic finesse with comic book slapstick… Children will love the mad jokes."
Guardian

Look out for the next story featuring Preston and friends, to be published in Collins Picture Lions in March 1998.